BEST OF BOTH WORLDS

N.R. WALKER

D1297258

BLURB

Sebastian Gilman meets a guy on a dance floor every Friday night. He knows nothing about him, not even his name, only to find one day this familiar stranger turns up on his building site and they need to work together.

Ryland Keller knows better than to get involved. Alone and half a country away from home, he revels in isolation until a handsome man in a gay bar turns his world upside down.

Sebastian wants to help Ryland recover from a horrible past, but only if Ryland can let his guard down long enough to see that he can have the best of both worlds.

This 20,000-word story is told in drabbles: each chapter consisting of only 100 words.

COPYRIGHT

Warning

Intended for an 18+ audience only. This book contains material that maybe offensive to some and is intended for a mature, adult audience. It contains graphic language, explicit sexual content, and adult situations.

Trigger warnings:

Mentions of violence and homophobia. Reader discretion advised.

BEST OF BOTH WORLDS

N.R. WALKER

PART ONE

THE LIGHTS ARE STROBING, the bass is thumping. Bodies are swaying, grinding, sweating.

I'm lost in a sea of metaphorical white and blue collars, from lawyers and doctors to tradesmen like me. Status isn't important on the dance floor. We're all accepted here: LGBT, proud and sensual. Sexual.

Hands and mouths push and pull, give and take, want and need.

I see him and he looks at me with those blue eyes that have owned me every Friday night for the last four weeks.

My hands are on his hips. He licks the sweat off my neck, and I shiver.

AS A CARPENTER, a contractor, I hide who I really am. But I love my job. My boss, Daevyn, respects me. He's a good man. Sometimes I think he might know the secret I keep, but he says nothing.

Other men I work with work hard, drink hard. They live for weekends: beer, football and women.

"Come on, Sebastian, we'll show you how real men drink," Jason scoffs.

Four o'clock Friday is tools down, beers up, but not for me. I have somewhere else I'd rather be. A dance floor with a blue-eyed guy whose name I do not know.

I ARRIVE with my friends and they know who I'm looking for. The mystery of this nameless stranger plagues me.

The dark club is alive with music and men. He's not

there and I am disappointed, but I drink and dance regardless.

A hand grabs my shoulder, pulling me around, and it's him. The guy I was dancing with no longer exists because blue eyes are an inch from mine. "You're late," I say.

He smirks and his sky-colored eyes shine. I lean close and ask him, "What's your name?"

He licks his lips. "Isn't it more fun not knowing?"

THE DEADLINE at work is brought forward and Head Office says to expect a new crew on Wednesday.

The construction company I work for is big, with dozens of subcontracted building teams across Seattle and the Northwest. Teams often work together to get jobs done.

I get to work on Wednesday with the sunrise and my heart stops.

There's a tall, brown-haired man with his back to me talking on his cell. Boots, strong lean legs, tool belt at his waist. He turns as he hears me and his voice trails away...

He stares at me with his sky-blue eyes.

"HAVEN'T GOT ALL DAY," Daevyn barks at us and our locked stare is broken. There are other construction workers buzzing around, though nobody seems to have noticed the lack of oxygen in the room.

We work the same site, but not together, and I catch myself looking around for him. Sometimes I swear I can feel his eyes on me, burning the skin on the back of my neck, on my blond hair.

On Thursday, I try to be near him, accidentally on purpose. He ignores me.

On Friday, still no words are spoken. I still don't know his name.

———

FRIDAY NIGHT, I scan the crowded club until closing time, but he doesn't show.

I wonder if it's because it's too real, too close to his real life. I wonder if he's out, if his family knows he's gay, or curious at least. I wonder if *he* knows it.

Or maybe there's someone else?

Is that why?

I realize I know nothing of this man, not even his name.

My friends have gone from saying, "You two are so hot on the dance floor. We see the way he looks at you," to saying, "Maybe it wasn't meant to be."

———

ON MONDAY, he's there early, though he looks tired, like he had a rough weekend.

I am determined to talk to him, to at least ask him... something.

Blue eyes that have haunted me for weeks flicker to mine and I can see him swallow. I grab the blueprints and walk directly over to him. "Can I have a second?"

I lay the plans out over the makeshift table, away from

listening ears, and I can feel him beside me. To others, it would look as though we're talking work, but instead I ask him, "Where were you on Friday?"

HE DOESN'T ANSWER my question, so I talk instead. "I know I don't know the first thing about you, but maybe we could start as friends."

My words aren't coming out right so I stop and start again. "I thought there was something... chemistry. I thought we had chemistry."

He's silent for too long and the knots in my stomach tighten. I pick up the plans and turn to leave when someone calls out, "Sebastian," and my head turns at my name.

I swear I hear him whisper, though it is to himself, not me. "Sebastian."

It makes me shiver.

I DO my best to avoid him for the rest of the week, though it's difficult and I can feel him looking at me. His eyes are like imaginary fingers, burning painlessly across my skin.

Sometimes when there's no one else around he looks like he might say something, but he doesn't.

By Friday, I am pissed off and frustrated. The guys ask me to join them for a drink, but I decline again. Jason, the Neanderthal he is, hollers, "Need some pussy, Gilman?"

Most of the boys laugh, except for one blue-eyed man, who pretends he didn't hear.

I STALK THROUGH THE CLUB, wearing jeans that hug my thighs and ass just right, and the green shirt that matches my eyes. I'm on a mission tonight to get drunk and to get laid.

Not my usual MO, but I'm sick of the games.

I need to forget.

I'm buzzed and dancing with Marcel, a French guy I've danced with before. I grind against his ass and I know I'm being watched.

I search the crowd until I find him. Sky-blue eyes are watching me dance with another man. His jaw is clenched and his chest is heaving.

MARCEL PRESSES his ass against me, an offering. His head falls back against my shoulder, his eyes are closed, and he moans.

But my gaze is on the man with sky-colored eyes, who is staring right at me. He looks a mixture of angry, disappointed, and turned on.

Keeping our gazes locked, I smile at him and bite down on the neck in front of me. His blue eyes close and his nostrils flare.

When his eyes shoot open again, they are different. Clearer. Determined. He crosses the dance floor to stand in front of me. And he stares.

MARCEL LOOKS AT HIM, challenging. "Can I help you?"

Blue eyes never leave mine. He answers low but direct. "Yes. You can leave."

My hands fall from Marcel's hips and he turns to look at me, to gauge my reaction. Marcel can see how intently we are staring at each other, this gorgeous familiar stranger and me. There's no competition. Marcel knows it. He huffs and walks away.

The brown-haired man with the sky-blue eyes steps forward, pressing the entire length of his body against mine.

And he whispers in my ear, a Southern-accented melody, "My name is Ryland."

RYLAND...

The feel of him against me sets my blood on fire. The music pounds in my chest and I grab his waist and grind against him. Ryland...

His fingers dig into me, his hip bone strokes my cock and we're not in a crowded sea of dancing bodies any more.

We are alone. Just me and him. Ryland...

His breath on my skin heats me, his lips at my ear ignite me.

The rest of the world falls away. We are the only two men on the face of the planet in that moment, just me and him. Ryland...

I TRAIL my lips up his neck and I can feel him shiver. I run my nose along his jaw and his breath stops in his throat. He gasps like he's drowning.

Finally, *finally*, my lips find his and I kiss him... hard.

One hand on the small of his back pulls him into me. My other hand wraps around his neck and jaw and pulls his mouth against mine.

I taste him, drink him and devour him. Ryland...

He pulls away too soon, to breathe it would seem. He grabs my hand and drags me off the dance floor.

HE PULLS me into a dark corner where the music is not so loud. His body is still against me; my hands are holding him there.

"I'm a little drunk," I tell him.

"I know," he answers.

"My name is Sebastian Gillman."

He smiles. "I know."

"I'm gay."

He laughs. "I know."

"You have a Southern accent," I tell him.

He snorts. "I know."

"You ignored me. You acted as if you didn't even know me," I tell him. "Like what we do here means nothing."

He no longer smiles. "I know."

I have to know. "Why?"

"I don't know."

CONFUSION, hurt and too many drinks fuel my fire. My voice is louder than I intended. "You *don't know?*"

His eyes dart to mine, my abrupt tone surprising him. He takes a step back from me and I immediately regret my outburst.

But something flares in his beautiful eyes and his tone matches mine. "Because I don't want *them* to know!"

And I suddenly feel very sober. He pulls at his hair and looks like he's ready to bolt so I grab a fistful of his shirt and I nod.

His voice is softer. "I won't go through that again."

IT'S TOO LOUD, too dark, and too hot. I need fresh air. Ryland seems to understand because when I pull on his hand and walk us to the exit he doesn't object.

The cool night air and the sounds of the darkened city are a welcome relief.

I still have his hand in mine and turn to face him. His eyes have lost some shine.

"Ryland, I understand, believe me I do," I say honestly. "The guys I work with don't know about me either."

His eyes dart to mine and he looks... scared.

"Ryland, they don't need to know."

I CAN SEE confusion and hesitation in those piercing eyes, like shards of ice, but there is a glimmer of resilience, of hope. It's there, I can see it.

I tell him I know that being a construction worker comes with certain stereotypes. "How's that for fucking irony?" I ask him.

I do my job. I'm fucking good at my job. Who I have sex with—who I fall in love with—is none of their business. It's none of their goddamn business. It shouldn't matter. It *doesn't fucking* matter.

Ryland waits for my rant to finish and then smiles.

"CAN WE GRAB SOME COFFEE?" he asks. It's after midnight and we're standing in the street outside the nightclub.

"Absolutely," I tell him. "My place isn't far." My words make me pause, knowing what I'd implied, and I rephrase my offer. "Or we can find a diner...?"

He smirks at my sudden shyness, so I explain. "I don't want you to think I'm inviting you to my place for sex. That's not what I meant, I just want to talk."

Ryland looks a mix of cautious and curious. His tone is casual when he asks, "Walking distance or taxi?"

I GIVE a tour of my house while we wait for the coffee machine to heat. I explain not all the rooms are finished. It's a work in progress.

An older-style bungalow in need of repair, it's my pride and joy, my home. I show him the back deck, though it's only half done. "It's slow because I'm doing it by myself and I'm rather particular about quality."

He inspects the framed family pictures and in twenty minutes he knows so much about me. My home, my family. I'm an open book to him.

"So, Ryland, tell me about you."

———————

HE'S UNEASY, not sure what to give away.

We sit on the sofa sipping coffee and I tell him it's okay, he can tell me when he's ready.

He tells me he tried to stay away from me, my blond hair and brown eyes, but failed. He says when he saw me dancing with another guy he made a decision right then and there, to *not* stay away from me anymore.

But then his voice is low when he tells me, "My choice to live my life, to not lie about myself or to myself anymore —to come out—cost me everything."

———————

HE LEAVES it at that and I don't push him. I tell him I'm sorry. It shouldn't be that way. It shouldn't make a difference, and it's wrong that it does.

He nods and looks at me with those damn eyes.

"Prettiest blue eyes?" He laughs and I realize then that I've said this out loud.

"Your eyes have haunted me for the last five weeks," I tell him.

He smiles kinda shyly and he's quiet, like he's about to say he has to leave.

I say the first thing that spews from my brain, just one terrifying word.

"Stay."

———

HIS EYES widen and I am quick to explain. "You can take the spare bed or the sofa. I just don't want you to leave."

He looks uncomfortable, so I add, "I can call you a cab if you'd prefer."

He waits before he speaks, to torture me I'm sure. Then he prods the cushion on the sofa and says, "Feels comfy enough."

I smile and show him the guest room. He stands at the door, his body so close to mine.

Seconds pound out like the heart in my chest. I want to kiss him so fucking much but I don't.

———

MY BODY'S conditioned to wake early whether I want it to or not. My eyes blink open at six AM and my brain kicks into gear.

I remember that Ryland slept in the spare room, but I doubt he's still there. I hope he is, but I won't be surprised to find him gone.

His door is open, the bed rumpled, the room empty. Disappointment lumps in my stomach and I head to the bathroom when I hear a distinct, "Ow, fucker."

I stick my head into the kitchen. I think he's killed my espresso machine, but I smile anyway.

———

WEARING his jeans from last night—no shirt, no shoes—he holds part of the coffee machine with one hand and inspects the fingers on his other.

I walk up beside him and he jumps at my sudden appearance. Flipping the faucet on, I run his fingers under cold water. I know he's touched the metal part that burns because I've done the same thing before.

"I wanted to make you coffee," he says. The gesture warms my heart. "Think I broke your machine."

Still holding his hand under the water, I smile at him. "I'm just glad you stayed."

HE LAUGHS at the burns across the top of his fingers and his Southern accent lures me in. We talk well into morning. It's easy. Actually, it's better than easy...

It's perfect.

He stands on my back deck discussing the work I've done and the work I've got to do. When he's talking my trade, he uses his hands to describe the pictures he sees in his mind so I can see them too.

I find myself in front of him, absorbed in his oh-so-blue eyes. His tongue swipes his bottom lip and it steals the breath from my lungs.

THOSE DAMN BLUE EYES. They get me every time.

I don't want to rush him. On the dance floor the last five Friday nights he's been brave and demanding, but he's cautious in the light of day and I can't say I blame him.

I want to touch him, to kiss him. God, I want to *have* him. But I don't want to rush him. And he can see that I'm torn.

"Sebastian," he says with a laugh. "Just fucking kiss me."

I chuckle, a little embarrassed. But I kiss him. Sweet God in heaven, do I kiss him.

———

"WHAT DO WE DO ON MONDAY?" he asks. His voice is so unsure. "At work, I..."

"I will be me. You will be you," I say. "Nothing has to change."

He nods, but he's not convinced.

"Look, Ryland, you don't have to tell me what happened, what's got you so scared, but you *can* trust me."

He looks at me with those imploring eyes.

I remind him, "We're keeping the same secret."

He leans over and kisses me, lightly, sweetly. He smiles and says, "Thank you, Sebastian."

He leaves then, and I am perplexed by this man. Confounded, intrigued, enamoured...

———

I'M nervous going to work on Monday, but I'm also eager to see him again. He's there when I arrive and his shoulders stiffen slightly when one of the guys he's talking to asks me about last night's game.

I tell Sam he'd feel a lot better when asking about football results if he followed the right team. The others laugh and Ryland smiles and visibly relaxes.

At lunch, someone asks Ryland about his bandaged fingers. He shrugs like he couldn't care less, but he smiles when he says, "Burned 'em."

I fight a grin until knock-off time.

HE'S at work all week and although we don't work in the same team, I am constantly aware of him.

He comes over on Wednesday night. We grab some pizza and beer and watch hockey re-runs. He kisses me, aligns our bodies, and his desire presses hot and hard against mine.

When he tells me he should go, my head falls back and I groan. He laughs, but he hisses when he adjusts his all-too-evident hard-on.

We've not progressed further than kissing but by the time Friday rolls around, I am desperate to get him back on the dance floor.

THE CLUB IS as it always is, but it feels different this time because I walk in holding Ryland's hand. And the usual crowd of guys notice.

I can't help but smile as they watch us. When I see my friends Neil and Brandon, they grin at me. I make introductions and Neil sighs dramatically. "It's about fucking time you two got together."

Ryland chuckles and after a few drinks and some laughs with them, Ryland looks toward the dance floor.

"For God's sake, Sebastian, dance with your boy," Brandon says with a laugh.

I smile and oblige, of course.

RYLAND EDGES his thigh in between mine and he starts to dance. It's a pulsing, swaying, grinding dance. His hands are on my hips and his lips are on my neck.

A shiver runs from my scalp to my toes and I welcome the onslaught of sensation.

I am lost to him: his hands, his breath on my skin, the way his cock rubs against my hip.

I kiss him, open-mouthed and swirling tongues, and he's holding me tighter and he grinds harder.

I kiss down his jaw, nipping, licking the stubble. He groans out a whimper. "Please, Sebastian. Please."

WITH HIS CHIN clamped in my fingers, I turn his head and speak into his ear. "If I take you home, I will have you in my mouth. I will suck you. Do you want that?"

His body convulses and he nods, his face flush against mine.

I can feel his shallow breath. His heaving chest matches my own. He looks at me and his blue eyes are now black. Whether it's the lights or the lust, I can't tell.

His cheek is pressed to mine and when he speaks, his mouth moves against my lips. "Can I taste you too?"

RYLAND STANDS BEHIND ME, running his hands up the back of my thighs and over my ass as I fumble with the key in the lock. I laugh. It's a nervous sound, of anticipation and sexual energy about to burst.

Finally the door opens and we step inside. I turn and push Ryland against the wall, my mouth on his, my hands on his belt. I pull at it roughly until I find my prize.

He moans as I pump him. When I drop to my knees and take him into my mouth, he fists my hair and all but screams.

———

THE SOUNDS he makes nearly end me. Gravelly and raspy, he moans and his breath stutters. "Oh, Sebastian... oh, my God..."

His cock is beautiful, long, thick and uncut. I take all of him in and he guides my head with hands in long, deep strokes.

"God, Sebastian, yes," he groans out strangled words. "So close."

I suck him harder, cup his balls and he thrusts his cock down my throat. His desire and lust spurts hot and thick, and I swallow.

He convulses and bucks, then pulls me up and holds me against him while his orgasm high subsides.

———

I LEAD the way to my bedroom and he has a lazy smirk—a post-orgasm smirk—and he's beautiful.

Then I am naked on my bed and he eyes my cock like a starving man and whispers, "Fuck yes."

Licking and nipping and squeezing and tasting, he teases me with his tongue and only when I am begging, does he take me into his mouth. He wraps his hands under my ass and pulls me down his throat.

I come so fucking hard and he moans as he drinks what I give. When my senses right themselves, he's wrapped himself around me.

WHEN I WAKE the next morning, he's still beside me. We're both naked and I admire his sleeping form: his perfect mouth, his muscular shoulders, his long legs.

Sleepy sky-colored eyes catch me. "Enjoying the view?"

I nod and he chuckles.

We shower together, both of us hard and aching, until we're back on my bed and both on our knees. Ryland strokes our cocks together and my tongue fucks his mouth in time with his hand.

I watch his face as he comes. Those eyes that own me flutter with lust and it spirals my orgasm with his own.

IT'S mid-morning and we're standing in my kitchen. He's wearing some of my clothes and it's like he can't stop touching me. His hand brushes mine, a caress of my hip, his breathy sighs into the back of my neck.

It's new but it's intimate. And very fucking good.

It's so easy between us, so easy and so very right.

But there's a loud knock at the door and Ryland's eyes widen as if he's been caught doing something he shouldn't.

A voice booms, "Sebastian, put your junk back in your pants and open the goddamn door."

I sigh. Fucking Hamish.

"IT'S OKAY, RY," I say quietly. "It's just my brother."

He's pale and quite frankly he looks scared. I cup my hand to his cheek and tell him, "You don't have to hide who you are with me. Work is different, I get that, but here, with my family, I am who I am."

Ryland swallows and breathes deeply, then finally he nods.

Hamish yells more profanities and I yell back at him to shut the fuck up. I unlock the door and he barrels through only to stop in his tracks when he sees that I am not alone.

HAMISH'S EYES flicker between us and the devil's grin spreads across his face. I'm watching Ryland's reaction to my hulk of a brother and Hamish says, "Well, shit, bro. I didn't know you had company."

I roll my eyes. "Would it have stopped you?"

"Uh, probably not," he says and proceeds to raid my fridge.

I stand near Ryland and feel him relax beside me. I tell Hamish with my eyes to be nice as I make introductions. Hamish just grins his stupid fucking grin and says, "Mom's gonna *fangirl* when I tell her Seb's got himself a man."

I CAN'T BELIEVE he just said that. Fuck me. "Did Annie kick you out?"

"Nuh," Hamish says, and he continues to scarf down three-day-old cold pizza.

"She should have," I tell him. Ryland is watching us and I can tell he doesn't know what to make of my brother.

"Next weekend," Hamish says, like he's just remembered, "Sunday lunch at Mom and Dad's."

Hamish plants himself on my sofa and starts flipping through sports channels on TV. I look at Ryland apologetically and he surprises me by smiling.

He sits down across from Hamish. "So, which game's on replay?"

I SIT NEXT TO RYLAND, my bare feet on the coffee table, and rub my thumb on his thigh where Hamish can't see. It's a reassuring gesture and I'm relieved when he smiles.

We talk about work and the ballgame, and I like that they get along. They both follow the Hawks and they give me hell, but I don't mind.

I don't mind at all.

When Hamish leaves, I don't get up to see him out. I tell him to shut the door behind him and when it closes, I have Ry on his back, pressed into the sofa.

THE NEXT WEEK at work is good. It's productive and we're making headway. The deadline will be an easy target.

On Tuesday night when Ry stays over, I ask about his family and he takes a while to speak. His answer is barely a whisper. "I have no family."

On Thursday night, I have dinner at Ry's apartment and I notice there are no photos of anyone. There's hardly any furniture. There's no history here.

I wonder what it is Ryland's not telling me, but I don't ask. He'll tell me when he's ready.

At least, I hope he will.

———

ON FRIDAY NIGHT, we arrive at the club, meeting Neil and Brandon at their usual table. Ryland seems distracted, like something's weighing on his mind. Like it's weighed on his mind all week.

When we're on the dance floor, his hands are on my hips and I look into his troubled blue eyes. "Ry, what's wrong?"

He shrugs it off, but I need to know. I kiss his lips lightly and tell him to please, please let me in.

He stops still and his hands drop from my body. His words pierce me. "Sebastian, I think we need to talk."

———

BACK AT MY HOUSE, he sits on my sofa with his head in his hands. Speaking quietly, I plead with him, "Ryland, if you don't want me, just tell me."

His eyes open wide and the fear is alarming. "What?

No! Sebastian, no!" He pushes his hand against his stomach, as if he's in physical pain. "I want to be with you. I want there to be an 'us,' but there's something I need to tell you. There's something you need to know."

I know he's been hurt. I'd gathered that much already.

I just had no idea how much.

"I WAS twenty when I met Brett," he explains. "I was still so unsure...but with him I couldn't deny I was gay. We had a... *secret affair*... we were lovers... for two years."

He's in front of me, vulnerable and raw. I hold his hand as he tells me, "But his family suspected something... and he left me."

"Oh, shit," I say. "I'm sorry."

"That's not the worst of it," he says with a frown. "My parents found out and they disowned me. The guys at work found out... and they bashed me to within an inch of my life."

TEARS POOL in his eyes when he talks. My heart breaks for him, my stomach somersaults to the floor.

"I spent a week in the hospital," he says, a fucked-up fact. "When I got out, I had nowhere to go. I took the first bus and it brought me here."

His hesitation to be open about himself, his fear of being found out becomes crystal clear.

I can't fathom his courage, his bravery, his strength to be

true to himself. I tell him this and wipe away his tears, and mine, and I hold him as tight as I can.

"THE INJURIES HEAL, YA KNOW," he murmurs. "The bones heal and bruises fade."

I run my fingers through his hair and kiss his face as he takes some deep breaths.

"But the wounds my parents... my brother... those wounds will never heal."

I tighten my hold on him. He fits against me just right.

"Being twenty-two and alone in the world is fucking scary as hell. All because of who I'm attracted to. The things they said, what they called me, Sebastian, I will never forget."

I wonder if he can feel my tears as they fall into his hair.

"I NEEDED TO TELL YOU," he says from the crook of my neck.

"Thank you for trusting me," I murmur.

He looks at me then and there's something unsaid in the stark blue of his eyes. I run my thumb across his cheek, gently, with love. "Ryland," I whisper. "You can tell me anything."

A dozen emotions flicker in his eyes before he looks away. "I needed to tell you because..."

He still won't look at me, so I ask, "Because?"

"Because you're the best thing in my life," he answers softly. "Because I want to give you my heart."

MY HEART POUNDS erratically in my chest, and I smile. I take his face in my hands and make him look at me. "Ry, my heart is already yours."

His brow furrows a little. His eyes are puffy but he grins. "Really?"

"Really." Then I whisper against his lips, "You're perfect, Ryland Keller."

"No, I'm not," he says, his knee-jerk reaction.

"You're perfect for me," I say before I kiss his eyelids, his temple.

He falls against me as though exhausted from carrying such a heavy weight for far too long. I take his hand and lead him to bed.

WITHOUT A WORD, I undress him. I pull his shoes and socks off and I press my lips to his toes. I take his jeans off and kiss his hipbone, then his shirt's gone and I kiss his chest.

He climbs into bed. I undress and join him, pulling him into my arms.

It's intimate, but it's not sexual. That's not what this is.

With his head on my chest, he holds onto me like I'd disappear if he didn't.

I run my fingers through his hair and press my lips to his forehead. "Sleep, Ry. I'm not going anywhere."

WHEN I WAKE, I find myself wrapped around Ryland, his back to my chest, his ass pressed against my cock.

I move my arm and try not to wake him, but he holds me in place and rubs his ass against my morning wood. I smile into his shoulder blade and he chuckles.

"Good morning," he mumbles.

"Yes, it is," I agree and kiss along his spine. He feels so good against me but I want to do this slowly. "Ry, I want take my time with you, all day, if you'll let me."

He moans and chuckles. "Starting with...?"

I GIVE him a hand-job in the shower, his hands and forehead against the tiles while I pump him from behind. Then I wash him, paying particular attention to his ass, pushing a fingertip in his hole, just enough to tease him.

He cooks breakfast and I massage the muscles in his shoulders, rubbing down to the backs of his thighs.

All day, I touch him, kiss him, trail my tongue along his jaw and whisper in his ear all the things I'll do to him.

By mid-afternoon, I have him so pliable that he shivers when I touch him.

HE'S ON MY BED. His engorged dick leaks precome onto his stomach. I've slipped another finger into him and he's begging incoherently.

He's so fucking beautiful, how he reacts to my touch, how he pleads my name.

Then I'm inside him, slowly, heavenly.

His legs wrap around me and I am so far inside him, his body slick and hot. Ryland, this man who has my heart, who's given me his, owns my body and soul.

I kiss him and the dual sensation of having my cock and my tongue so thoroughly inside him sends my orgasm into a spin.

―――

HIS HEAD IS THROWN BACK, his chest pressed into mine, and he grunts through gritted teeth. Ryland bucks underneath me and his swollen cock, sandwiched between us, pulses and spills violently.

His ass clenches my cock and I can't fight it anymore. I fuck hard for two, three thrusts and I surge inside him. The pleasure runs in liquid fire from my bones and fills the condom.

Emotions overtake me, then his arms are around me and I'm almost sobbing into his neck.

Ryland lifts my face so he can see my eyes, and he whispers, "I love you too."

―――

WE ARRIVE AT MY PARENTS' house and I park behind my brother's car. I'm excited, but Ryland's nervous so I take a moment to squeeze his hand and recap my earlier explanations. "Remember what I said about my mother... she's gonna hug you. Be prepared for that. My sister Gabby will give you fifty questions. Ignore her."

He smiles at me, but I keep going. "You've met Hamish. His wife Annie is great, she'll love you."

"And your dad?" he asks quietly.

"What? The ringleader of this circus? Come on," I say, getting out of the car. "I'm starving."

I TOLD him he didn't have to come to my parents' place, but he said he wanted to. Standing at their front door, he's hesitant. He's pushing his boundaries, for himself and for me.

I ask him again if he's sure. He lost his family because he's gay, yet here he stands, about to meet mine—as my boyfriend. He nods.

He must be so far out of his comfort zone, I can't even imagine. I squeeze his hand and we walk inside.

"Oh, thank God," Hamish cries. "Ryland, get over here. Hawks are two down, I need some moral support."

"I DON'T GO to a hairdresser, Gabby," I say again. "I go to a barber."

She shakes her head at me. "You're a disgrace to gay men everywhere, Sebastian."

I roll my eyes and Ryland chuckles beside me. I pick up dirty plates off the table and take them to the sink. Ryland follows me, carrying some trays. "Your family's great."

"They like you," I say and lean toward him, capturing his lips with mine.

Mom walks in and Ryland jumps back. "S-s-sorry," he stammers.

Mom pats his arm and says, "You can kiss him, Ryland. He *is* kinda cute."

RYLAND BLUSHES as my father walks in, smiling. He collects three beers from the fridge, hands one to Ryland, then me, and says, "Allison, leave the boys alone."

Mom huffs but smiles and Dad asks Ryland if she's hugged him yet. She gives Dad the stink-eye and I laugh.

As we're leaving, Mom tries to contain herself but makes a squeaking sound. Ryland can see she's about to burst if she doesn't hug him, and he gives her a small nod. She pulls him in and hugs him, hard. Everyone chuckles and Mom beams.

Ryland smiles the entire way home.

WORK IS WRAPPING UP, our last week at this site. My last week of working with Ryland, seeing him every day: his brown hair and blue eyes, that sexy smile, his legs in work boots, his tool belt on his hips.

At dinner on Tuesday night, his cell phone rings. It's an unknown number. "Hello?" There's silence on the line. "Hello?" No one speaks. The line clicks dead and Ry shrugs. "Must have been a wrong number."

On Friday night he tells me that number calls him every day. No one speaks, but he thinks he knows who it is.

WE SPEND the next weekend at my house. We work on the back deck, make out on the sofa, and make love in my bed.

He leaves some clothes at my place, a toothbrush and razor in the bathroom, some of his granola in the pantry.

It makes sense. He's here more than he is at his own place and I like seeing reminders of him when he's gone. Finding his shirt with mine makes me smile.

His phone rings again on Saturday, but he doesn't answer it. "Ry?" I ask.

He replies, "I have nothing to say to him."

———

"I THINK IT'S JUSTIN... my brother," he says. "There was a voice in the background that sounded like Kate. She called him 'sugar.' She's always called him 'sugar.'"

"Did he say anything?" I ask.

He shakes his head. "No, the line went dead."

He tries to convince me it doesn't bother him, but I can see it does. His sky-blue eyes are overcast and troubled.

"Have you tried calling him?" I whisper.

"It's been two years. He stood with my parents when they told me they only had one son." His eyes are a haunting blue. "I have nothing to say."

———

"I'M GOING to miss seeing you every day," he says. We're naked in bed. "Even if it is just at work."

An answer to our problem occurs to me. "Move in with me."

He freezes for a second, his eyes are wide. "Sebastian..."

I tell him, "You'd pay rent, half the utilities and food. You'd have your room, your bed. You basically live here anyway."

"Can I think about it?"

"Of course," I reply. Then I tap my fingers on his hip and count to five. "Done thinkin' yet?"

He laughs, and rolls us over so I'm under him.

ON TUESDAY NIGHT when his phone rings, caller ID shows it's a number he doesn't want to answer. He lets it ring but he's breathing harder and when it rings again, he hands it to me.

"Hello?" I say.

There is silence on the line. I think my voice has thrown him. But it's me who gets thrown for a loop when a female voice speaks. "Ryland?"

"No. It's Sebastian."

"My name is Kate, please don't hang up," she pleads. "Is Ryland there?"

Ryland shakes his head.

"He doesn't want to talk to you," I say, and end the call.

RY FALLS asleep and I watch him. He's restless; old wounds are open anew.

Friday is our last day on-site. The boys are keen for a drink, but I wish them well, shake hands and say it's been great. I leave, knowing Ry won't be far behind.

He's been quiet these last few days and I know what's on his mind.

We skip the club, opting for pizza and beer at his place. We're laughing as we walk up to his door and there are two people in the hall.

Ryland stops walking and the pizza falls to his feet.

THEY FACE us and Ryland takes a step back. I stand in front of him, putting myself between him and them, whoever they are.

I notice the woman first. She's young and pretty with blonde hair. She raises her hand in peace, looks at me, then to the man behind her.

Then I notice him. He's tall, with short black hair. He appears non-threatening, in fact he seems anxious.

He steps toward us and Ryland sucks in a ragged breath behind me. The stranger's standing in the light now. I can see his face clearly.

And he has sky-colored eyes.

RYLAND GRABS the back of my shirt and I can hear his shallow breaths. "What do you want?" I ask them, though I'm fairly sure I know.

The woman speaks first. "Are you Sebastian? I'm Kate, this is Justin."

Ryland's voice is small and strangled. "Why? Why are you doing this?"

Justin answers. His voice desperate. "Because you're my brother, I love you, and I'm so fucking sorry."

A tortured sob rips from Ryland's chest and I can feel him shaking. I pull him against me and he seems to breathe easier.

"Just hear me out," Justin says. "Please... please."

RYLAND LOOKS AT ME, his stark blue eyes asking me what he should do.

"Whatever you want," I tell him. He closes his eyes and nods, and with shaking hands, he opens his apartment door.

I pick up the dropped pizza and walk in first. Ryland follows and holds the door open. It's an invitation that Justin and Kate don't knock back.

Sitting in his small living room, no one speaks for a long while. I can see Ryland's hurt is quickly becoming anger and finally he snaps. "You've got ten seconds, Justin. Fucking talk or leave."

"I'M SORRY," Justin blurts out. "I'm sorry I didn't speak up, I'm sorry you left. I'm sorry you felt you had to."

"*Felt* I had to?" Ryland cries. "They kicked me out!"

"I know," Justin says. Kate squeezes his hand. "I'm sorry I never came to see you at the hospital."

"I had the ever-loving shit kicked outta me, Justin. I nearly died." Tears pool in his eyes. "*No one* came to see me."

"I'm sorry," Justin repeats. "I was young and stupid. I'm sorry."

Silence booms then Ryland's voice is almost inaudible. "Do Dad and Momma know you're here?"

JUSTIN'S SILENCE is his answer and Ryland's face twists. He stands up, and pulls at his hair. "Why are you doing this to me?"

Justin stands then, and when they're close it's easy to tell they're brothers, even though Ryland's hair is dark brown, Justin's is black, and they have different-shaped faces. I wonder which parent they look like, if it's their mom or dad who has those crystal-blue, ever-seeing eyes.

Justin pounds his chest. "Because if I had to choose," he says, wiping away his tears, "if I had to pick between them and you, Ry, I'd choose you."

THEY STAND, face to face, and Ryland heaves a wracking sob. He half leans forward, like his lungs won't take oxygen, and his brother wraps his arms around him.

Ryland falls into him. He's taller and older, but he crumples into his younger sibling and it's torture to watch. And beautiful, it's so beautiful.

Kate, who I'd almost forgotten about, throws her arms around me. She sobs and mumbles an apology about putting snot on my shirt.

I hear Ryland chuckle and then Kate hugs him so hard. Ryland's eyes eventually open and he looks at me.

IN TWO STEPS, he's beside me. His arms slide around me in a side-on kind of hug. I kiss the side of his head and rub his back. He nods against my neck.

Justin looks at us, and smiles. "You must be Sebastian."

I nod and he nods, and everyone takes some much-needed deep breaths. I look at Ryland and say, "You have a lot to talk about. Would you like me to go?"

"No," Ryland and Justin answer together.

We both look at Justin and he explains, "You have more right to be here than me. Please stay."

JUSTIN AND KATE have four more days in Seattle before they have to head home. They talk openly, honestly. It's not easy, there is so much heartache between them, but it's progress.

It's slow, it's hard on Ry, but it's progress.

Kate and I give them space, leaving to grab some coffee. "You have no idea how happy Justin is now Ryland's talking to him, at least," she offers.

"It's good for Ryland," I reply. "Just don't push him too hard."

Kate nods and I press the issue. "I don't think any of us will fully understand what Ry's been through."

"HE'S STRONG," I tell Kate, "the strongest person I know, but if this ends badly, I don't think he'll recover."

We pick up our coffees and head back. "Justin's been a mess for so long without him," Kate says. "I think he'll take whatever part Ryland will give of himself." Kate smiles sadly and says, "Justin would've been happy to just see him alive and well. He said he'd sleep better if he just knew his brother was okay." Kate smiles at me warmly then. "But he's better than okay and Justin knows he has you to thank for that."

RYLAND EXPLAINS how he lived in a hostel when he first arrived, bruised and battered. When his bones healed, he found work and eventually saved enough to get his own place.

He was too scared to make any friends, his faith and trust in others was gone.

He'd seen an ad for a gay club downtown and it took him weeks to find the courage to go.

He smiles when he admits he used to watch a tall, good-looking guy with sand-colored hair. He smiles at me. "I watched him for weeks before I had the courage to dance with him."

"I TRIED to hide the real me," Ry says. Then he laughs. "It was weeks before I told him my name."

I grin at him and he slides into my embrace. Ryland looks at his brother, who is watching us. "Justin, I'm done hiding," Ry says. "This is who I am. If you don't like that, then tough. I won't hide anymore."

He knows now that he's worth it. He's confident enough

in himself, and in me, to look his brother in the eye and tell him outright.

I am so proud of him. This is his moment and he shines.

WHEN IT'S time for Justin and Kate to leave, it's a happy goodbye. They still have some issues to resolve, but there are happy tears, promises of phone calls and visits.

Justin hugs his brother for the longest time and Ryland somehow seems taller.

Then Justin thanks me and hugs me until Ryland taps our shoulders and tells us we've hugged enough. "He's mine," Ry growls. Justin laughs.

Later that night, I'm taking a shower when Ry barges in, like something just couldn't wait. "Life's too short," he says. "If the offer still stands, I wanna move in with you."

I LOOK into his eyes and there is no hesitation. No doubt. "Of course, anything you want."

I pull him into the shower even though he's fully dressed. He laughs. When he's finally naked, I turn and press my ass against his hardening dick.

It's an offering and he knows it. His hands stop on my hips and he whispers into my shoulder, "Sebastian, are you sure?"

I nod, but he needs to hear me say it. So I turn in his arms and kiss him. "Ryland, I'm certain. I want you. I want you to have me that way."

I SHUT the water off and he dries me. He takes me to bed and he takes his time, covering every inch of me with his hands and his mouth.

He's so in tune with my body—the sounds I make, how I move—and when he's finally inside me, he's gentle, so sure, so deep.

He lights fireworks with his long slow strokes and I'm so close, so fucking close.

Strong, calloused hands cup my face, his forehead rests on mine and when his flame-blue eyes ignite, my body reacts and an orgasm like no other spills between us.

HE LOOKS at me in wonder, with love and lust in his eyes as my mind floats back into my boneless body. He pulls my knee up to his shoulder and he shudders and groans and his jaw is clenched tight.

His head falls back and it's a sacred, *sacred* sound he makes when his body stills over mine, inside mine. I've witnessed something beautiful, something just for me.

He pulls out and takes care of me. I fall asleep in strong arms with kisses in my hair, and a sweet Southern voice whispering about having the best of both worlds.

THREE WEEKS LATER, Mom and Dad arrive at our place. Mom's carrying a box, a house-warming gift, she says. I shake my head and object. "This isn't a house-warming."

"It is now that Ryland lives here," she counters. I can't disagree.

The back deck is now done—the laundry is next—and we sit there, my family complete, enjoying the last of the summer sun.

Ryland opens the gift. It's a new espresso machine and he laughs. Mom kisses his cheek and he grins beautifully. "Thank you," he says and she hugs him. "Thank you, so much. For accepting me. For everything."

PART TWO

Six months later, Ryland and Sebastian still have the best of both worlds... until Ryland gets a phone call that changes everything.

WE ARRIVE at the club before Neil and Brandon. What had been a group of three friends for years is now four. After only six months, they include Ryland in our circle of friends like he's the missing piece.

Neil throws his arms around Ry the second he sees him, Ry smacks him on the ass and orders him to the bar. Brandon laughs, already scouting the club for his next twink conquest, and Ryland shakes his head at him.

It's like it's been the four of us forever.

We joke and laugh, drink and dance, and life's pretty fucking sweet.

———

NEIL HOOKS up with a guy he's seen a few times and he looks rather happy with himself. Brandon, true to form, finds himself a pretty young twink and they disappear unseen. He'll check in with one of us tomorrow; he always does.

Ry and I cab it home. Ry is a happy drunk—he giggles and finds everything funny. Which is cute, and quite distracting during mutual blow jobs.

He's licking and chuckling, sucking and giggling and God only knows what's going through his mind.

But his laughter turns to moans when I take him deep in my throat.

———

IT'S BEEN six months since Ryland moved in with me, and I still smile when I wake to find him beside me.

He's sleeping, snuggled into the warm blankets, a gorgeous mess of brown hair and scruff.

His sky-blue eyes open slowly, making me smile. "Morning, beautiful."

He smiles right back, but pulls the blankets over his head. I join him under there, cocooned in our little world, and suck his nipple between my lips.

His cell phone interrupts us, and Ryland groans. Flipping the covers back, he reaches for the phone, checking the screen before answering.

"Justin, wassup?"

I CAN HEAR Ryland's brother talking through the phone, but I'm still paying attention to Ryland's chest and ribs with my mouth.

Ryland stills underneath me and taps my shoulder so I stop licking and look at him.

"When?" he asks. He nods, though Justin can't see him, and scrubs his hand over his face. "I don't know if I can," he says softly.

He's quiet for a while and it seems Justin isn't talking either. "I'll call you back," Ryland murmurs.

He ends the call and I ask him, "Ry? What's wrong?"

He clears his throat. "My father died."

OH, FUCK. "OH," I say, not sure what other words will do. "I'm sorry."

He doesn't respond. His arms are hiding his eyes and his face, and he says nothing. He doesn't move.

I slide up beside him and he finally shifts his arms. At

least I can see his face—blank, void of any emotion—and he blinks.

"Ry..."

He looks at me then, but before I can say another word, he's up and heading to the bathroom. I hear the shower start and I sit, unmoving on the bed, completely at a loss for what to do or say.

WHEN HE COMES OUT, he's dressed for work, like it's any other day. Except it's not. Because his father just died.

The father who disowned him. The father who never wanted to see him again. The father who called him a 'faggot' and 'queer' and kicked him out of the house.

The same father who refused to visit his son in the hospital, even though he very nearly died. That father, that man... The man who inflicted the worst kind of wound.

"Hey," I say and stand in front of him. "Take the day off. We'll stay here. Just us."

HE LOOKS as if he might object, and for a moment I think he will. But then he sags a little and I pull him into my arms.

He leans against me and he sighs. And finally he nods.

I make him coffee, we phone our bosses and request personal time off. He still doesn't say anything; he just sits on the sofa, turning his phone over in his hands.

He turns it on then off half a dozen times. "I have to call Justin," he says.

"I'll grab a shower," I tell him, "and give you some privacy."

WHEN I COME BACK OUT, Ry is still on the lounge. "What did Justin say?" I ask.

"It was a massive heart attack," he answers. "He thinks the funeral is next Tuesday."

I sit beside him and place my hand on his bouncing knee. It's a habit he has, to bounce his knee when his mind is working overdrive. His knee stills and his blue eyes dart to mine.

"Do you want to go?" I ask. "To the funeral?"

"What, to pay my respects?" he asks with a humorless laugh.

"No, Ry," I say quietly. "To say goodbye."

"WE CAN TAKE some days off and fly down," I suggest.

He shrugs and I don't push it. I tell myself he'll talk when he's ready. I kiss him and tell him I love him. His head falls against the back of the sofa. I hold his hand and he stares at me with those sky-colored eyes.

We don't need to use words right now. He just needs to know I'll be there, without words, without hesitation.

So I wait for him to talk. Because I'll always wait for him.

Finally he speaks. "I don't know how I should feel..."

"THERE'S no right or wrong way to feel," I try to reassure him. His father hurt him in ways I'll never comprehend, and the news of his death is sure to leave a hurricane of emotions. "If you want to go to the funeral, Ry, we can. If you don't, that's okay too. It's your choice, whatever you want to do."

He nods but says no more. I pull the quilt off our bed and we spend the day watching movies, with him in my arms.

He falls asleep, I pull my cell phone from my pocket and hit Call. "Mom?"

LATE AFTERNOON, Ry has woken from a few hours' sleep and reality has settled in. My parents arrive and no sooner is my mother in the house than she has Ryland in a crushing hug.

They know diluted details of Ryland's history, that he's talking again with his brother after two years' absence. But they don't know specifics.

It's a surprise at first, and in hindsight it shouldn't have been, but when Dad hugs Ryland, he hugs him back, hard.

Mom notices as well, and when Dad pulls Ry into the living room, Mom suggests I help her with dinner.

"LET THEM TALK," Mom whispers as we start preparing dinner.

My doctor father has an excellent bedside manner. He's calming, reassuring and empathetic. As a father, he's been supportive of all my decisions. His belief in owning your actions, whether right or wrong, makes him strict but fair.

If Ry needs a father figure to talk to, to get things right in his head, then my father is perfect.

My boyfriend, my partner, sees my father as someone he can talk to. And my father treats Ryland like a son.

Understanding, I nod at my mom, and she smiles.

DINNER IS ALMOST DONE when Ry and my Dad walk back into the kitchen. Ryland doesn't hesitate, he just walks straight up to me and puts his hands on my waist, his head on my shoulder. "Thank you," he whispers.

Dad smiles at me. I kiss Ry's temple and rub the small of his back. "Any time."

There's a knock at the door and my father lets Hamish and Annie in. Hamish wastes no time in hugging Ryland and before Ry can be overwhelmed or embarrassed at the attention, Annie kisses his cheek and tells him, "It's what families do."

"YOU'RE A HUGGY BUNCH," Ryland jokes. It's good to see him smile.

"It's hereditary," I tell him, and give a pointed nod to my mom and brother.

Ryland looks at me with his imploring blue eyes. "If I go to the funeral, will you come with me? It won't be a pleasant trip..."

"Of course," I answer immediately. Ryland smiles, almost relieved. "Anything for you." I tell him. "Anything."

He takes his phone to call his brother. When he's gone, I ask my father, "Will he be okay?"

Dad smiles at me. "He has you, son. He'll be just fine."

———————

WE WALK my family to the door, and they promise to call tomorrow. And I don't doubt they will.

We say goodbye and when it's just us, Ry stares at me. His eyes, those too-blue eyes, see into my very soul. Stepping closer to me, he fists my shirt and leans his forehead against my chin. "What would I do without you?"

I lift his face and press my lips to his. "We'll never have to find out."

His eyes close and I hold him and he mumbles into my neck, "Sebastian, please take me to bed. I need you..."

———————

HIS NEED and his emotions are so palpable; he holds me tighter, with his arms around my waist and his legs around my thighs. I am so deep inside him and we're rocking, a sensual ebb and flow.

I hold his face in my hands and his eyes are glued to mine, hooded but ever-seeing blue. I push farther into him and he takes me, all of me, and I can see his need staring back at me.

He needs this connection, this intimacy, this love. And I give it to him, until he's shaking, convulsing and spilling between us.

THE NEXT MORNING, I call my boss Daevyn and request a week's leave. "Everything okay?" he asks, and I reassure him it will be. Ryland organizes time off work, I book the plane tickets and Justin insists we stay with them.

Twenty-four hours later, we're boarding a plane for Texas.

Ryland's nervous, and truthfully so am I, but he tells me he needs to do this.

I haven't asked him what he spoke about with my father, but on the plane he tells me. "I told your dad everything," he says. "He knows what my father did, what he said."

I SQUEEZE his hand and he continues, "I told him I didn't understand why I felt the loss of my father... when I'd lost him years ago... it didn't make sense."

"Oh, Ry," I whisper, wishing I could pull him into my arms, but the damn seats on planes...

"He told me grief is a funny thing, never the same for any two people. He told me maybe I wasn't grieving the loss of my father as such, more the loss of the relationship we could never fix. I'm grieving the relationship I never had... and will now never have."

"YOUR DAD... YOUR PARENTS," he corrects himself. "Your whole family is pretty fucking great."

I give him a sad smile. "We had it so different, didn't we?"

He answers with a sarcastic huff. "How did your family take the news... when you told them?"

"That I was pursuing carpentry instead of becoming a doctor?" I ask with a grin. "My parents told me building family homes is an honorable job." But I know what he means, so I add, "I think my parents knew I was gay before I did." I squeeze his hand again. "They told me they'd love me regardless."

HE'S quiet for the rest of the trip, and I fear my words are the reason. He's lost in his thoughts and I wish he'd tell me how he feels.

We arrive in Texas and we're met by Justin, Kate and the Southern heat. Ryland and his brother embrace and Justin whispers words I can't hear. Ryland nods.

Over the last six months, there have been frequent phone calls and another visit. Ryland savors his relationship with his brother. His only family.

Kate slips her arm in mine. "How is he?"

I shake my head. "He's not doing so great."

RYLAND'S quiet on the drive to Justin and Kate's. He looks at the passing scenery and says not much has changed, when the truth is everything is different now.

We get to their house. They give us a tour and show us our room and we settle in for small talk. There's an elephant in the room and it's not until it's late that Ryland speaks of it. "How's Momma?"

Justin smiles a sad smile. "She's not so great. But she's a Keller, stubborn and proud."

I smile.

Justin looks at me and smirks. "Sound like someone you know?"

WHEN WE FINALLY CRAWL INTO bed, Ry is restless. I cup his cheek. He places his hand over mine and holds it there, tenderly, lovingly.

"How does it feel to be back here?" I ask.

He closes his eyes. "Last time I was here, I left with seven broken bones, a punctured lung, and I have no idea how many fractured bones in my hands. And alone. I left alone... I never thought I'd come back, not for anything."

Shuddering at the thought of what he's endured, I pull him against me. His breathing soon evens out and he sleeps.

JUSTIN LOANS US HIS MOTORCYCLE, which Ryland apparently knows how to drive. "Motorcycles aren't exactly compatible with Seattle weather," he says with a shrug.

He throws his leg over and pats the seat behind him. I climb on and rub myself against his ass. "Just like this?" I ask and he smiles.

He shows me the schools he went to, where he used to hang out, where he first realized he was gay.

It was a movie cinema, he was sixteen, and some girl had kissed him. I laugh at his expression. "It wasn't funny," he says, "it was wrong."

———————

ON THE DAY before the funeral, he takes me out of town. He takes the motorcycle down some fancy drive, pulls up and turns off the engine.

There's a grand old two-story house set back a few hundred yards away. Ryland just sits and stares at it.

He doesn't have to tell me. I can tell the way he looks at it, how he's taking quicker breaths. I'm still sitting behind him on the motorcycle so I tighten my arms around him and sigh into his shoulder.

He hasn't said as much, but I know... this is his family's home.

———————

"I WAS SUPPOSED to go to college to study architecture," he says, still looking at the house in front of us. "But my father insisted I learn from the ground up. He said I should be able to build what I design." He exhales loudly. "Obviously the dream of a college fund went out the window with the dream of the straight son."

I open my mouth to ask him if he still wants to go to college, but people walk out of the house toward their waiting cars, and Ry quickly starts the motorcycle and we are gone.

———————

THE NEXT MORNING, Ry is quiet. We're dressed in dark suits, funeral attire. I stand in front of him and when I cup his cheek, he leans into me.

He's about to say goodbye to a man he both hates and loves in equal measure. And to add insult to injury, he's not exactly welcome to do so.

I have no idea what we are about to face, how Ryland will be received, particularly with me, a man, by his side.

Some might call it stupidity, but I call it blind faith. And I walk with him into the unknown.

IT'S a graveside service and there are a lot of people. Ryland's happy to stand at the back, away from all the people. We can hear the minister sing the praises of Jim Keller: a good man, a family man.

It's blasphemy and a downright fucking lie.

But I say nothing.

I can see Ry is looking through the crowd. Strangers to me, but he's known them all his life.

Justin is standing next to Kate and a woman I presume to be Ryland's mother. Justin stares at Ryland as if he should be there beside him.

But he's not.

PEOPLE RECOGNIZE him and word spreads like Chinese whispers that Ryland's there. Heads turn, looking, until they find him.

"Are you okay?" I ask quietly.

His eyes meet mine, searching for what, I'm not sure, and he nods.

The service ends and people gather in circles, but Justin and Kate waste no time in coming over. Kate hugs Ryland first, then Justin does, and people start to talk. They stare at him as they leave.

"We're going back to Momma's," Justin says. "Will you come?"

Ry looks back to the open grave. "I have something I need to say first."

JUSTIN, Kate and I stay in the shade of the tree we've been standing under. We watch the whispering crowd as they watch Ryland walk toward the grave. He needs to talk to his father for the last time.

He stands alone, he doesn't speak out loud and he doesn't cry. But his hands open and close at his sides and my heart aches for him. I can only imagine the one-sided, silent conversation he's having.

He has had no closure, no rebuttal to his father's cruel words. Nothing. Just an open grave and words that go unspoken.

And unheard.

I WATCH HIM, I ache to be beside him, but he said he needs to do this on his own. He knows I'm not far away and that I'm watching.

It's then I notice a woman looking at him, *staring* like

she can't believe her eyes. It's the woman I presume to be his mother, by the way people surround her. But she's staring at Ryland.

Justin, who's standing beside me, is watching them too. He mutters, "Oh, Momma, please don't..."

Ryland turns and looks at her, and they both stare.

Without a single word, she turns and walks away.

RYLAND'S FACE FALLS, his shoulders slump and I can see him breathing hard. He walks back toward us, looking at the ground, taking mechanical steps.

He won't look at me and when I step closer to him, he flinches away. "Let's just go," he murmurs.

Justin and Kate drive us back to their house. No words are spoken. Ryland's hands are in his lap, and he doesn't offer one for me to hold. Before we get out of the car, Justin turns and says to Ryland, "I'll speak to Momma."

"No. Don't," Ryland whispers. "I think she made herself clear."

INSIDE THE HOUSE, Ryland is quiet. Too quiet. "Ry," I whisper to him.

"I'm gonna take a shower," he says, and the water runs well after it would have turned cold.

I stand in the backyard as the afternoon settles into dusk, trying to not let my thoughts darken any further. This is not about me, I know that. This is about Ryland—the loss of his father and the loss, all over again, of his mother.

I am lost in my thoughts and don't hear him come up behind me.

Silently, he leans his forehead against my back.

———————

I AM ALMOST SCARED to turn around, scared to push him, in case he turns away from me again. "You okay?" I ask softly.

He says nothing, but shakes his head against my back.

I turn then and quickly pull him against me. He falls into me and I wrap my arms around him.

And for the first time since the news of his father's passing, Ryland allows himself to cry.

His hands claw at my clothes, my skin, and he shakes and sobs. I do my best to hold him together while he falls apart in my arms.

———————

I RUB his back and hold his head against my chest as he cries. I can tell he's trying to control his breathing and he pulls away, scrubbing at his face.

"I'm sorry," he stammers.

"You never have to apologize to me," I tell him. "You've nothing to be sorry for."

My words bring fresh tears and heaving sobs, such unbearable grief. But moreover, he once again doubts himself, he doubts his self-worth.

So I lift his face in my hands and kiss his cheeks. I tell him I love him, and I can taste his tears on my tongue.

RYLAND CLINGS to me all night as he sleeps, and I do nothing but hold him tighter. He's restless and he mumbles in his sleep, words I can't make out. I rub circles on his back, running my hands through his hair and over his face.

But he wrestles with his demons. Even asleep he has no peace.

I finally sleep after two AM, and when I wake the next morning, I'm alone.

I get up to find Kate and Justin in the kitchen, and Ry sitting outside by himself in the morning sun with a coffee in his hand.

I CAN TELL Justin wants to talk to Ryland. He eyes him nervously. We're packed and ready to leave for the airport.

Justin exhales loudly. "Ry, Dad changed his will. He left the farm and some money to Momma." Justin whispers the rest. "But he left the rest to me."

His father's final words to Ryland sound in my head. *We only have one son.* Ryland's eyes fall and he nods.

"But Ry," Justin says, "I've told my lawyer you're to get half."

Ryland shakes his head. "No."

"Please, Ry, it's only right," Justin pleads. "I won't lose you twice."

KATE CUPS her hands around Justin's face. "You're a good man, Justin Keller."

Ryland walks to the back door and he stops, but says nothing.

"Ry," I say quietly. He hears me, I know he does, but he walks out anyway.

Justin tells me to give him time. "Let him get his head around it."

So I pack our bags into the car and busy myself, trying to act like I'm okay.

But I'm really not. My heart is heavy, leaden, aching. Loneliness and dread settle in my chest. Ryland won't look at me now, and distance sits between us.

WE GET home to Seattle and Ryland never mentions his father's money or his mother's rejection. The absence of this conversation is a festering wound and I am helpless to watch it grow.

I try to broach the subject, but Ryland ignores me, like he doesn't hear my words. But I know he does. I see the flicker of hurt and fear in his sad blue eyes before he turns away.

So I leave the subject alone. I tell myself he needs time, that he'll be okay, that we'll be okay.

But the divide between us is fast gaining ground.

WE'VE BEEN BACK in Seattle for a week when Mom and Dad visit. Mom hugs Ryland as she always does, but he doesn't hug her back.

Dad says quietly, "I assume things didn't go well..."

"No," Ryland says flatly. "My father is still dead. And my mother still only has one son." Grabbing his keys, Ryland walks out and mumbles he'll be back.

My parents look at me, stunned. "He won't talk to me," I admit.

"Give him time," Dad says.

"I'll give him anything he needs," I say, trying not to cry. "But he won't even look at me."

TIME. He needs time. Give him time. Everyone says it.

Well, time I have. Countless hours of time, of loneliness, of silence, of staring at the ceiling, praying for sleep. Ryland lies on his side, facing away from me, and the cold divide between us grows.

I long to hold him, just hold him... but the fear of rejection, of pushing too hard, stops me.

So I whisper that I love him.

He pretends he's asleep, but his shallow breathing tells me he's not. And in the morning, as every day for the last two weeks, I wake up alone.

MY BOSS DAEVYN asks me if everything's okay. I shrug. "Sure."

He looks around, then at me, long and hard. "Everything okay with whatshisname?" he asks.

I stare at him then, and I know that he knows. I'd always suspected he did.

"I've known you since you were a first-year apprentice, Gilman. I saw how you looked at him," he says. "It don't bother me none. What you do in your bedroom is nobody's business."

I open my mouth to speak, but words fail me.

"Do you need any time?" he asks.

I bark out a laugh. Time. Motherfucking time.

I GET HOME HAVING DECIDED NOT to tell Ryland that not only does Daevyn know I'm gay, he knows Ryland is too.

I can't risk scaring Ryland further away, giving him ammunition in his civil war. So I say nothing.

But I'm determined to try to save us. He gets home not long after me and he walks in keeping his eyes on the floor.

I walk right up to him and tell him, "I'm not leaving you."

His sky-blue eyes close as I press my lips to his forehead. He doesn't pull away from me, and it's a start.

HE WATCHES television and I go to bed alone. Exhausted, I sleep and in the morning, he's gone before me.

I walk slowly into the kitchen. My heavy heart burns. But he's put my coffee mug out for me, and the espresso machine is set to warm.

It's silly, nothing monumental, but he did it for me. He thought of me.

I smile.

I go to work, minding my own, but happier. I'm busy for an hour or so, until Daevyn yells, "Gilman!" across the worksite. He has his phone to his ear and his eyes tell me something's wrong.

"THERE'S BEEN AN ACCIDENT," he tells me, "at the Watchman site. The Keller kid's been hit by a van. You better get to the hospital."

I don't remember leaving and I don't remember driving. The next thing I know, I'm at the emergency department and the triage nurse won't let me in. I'm not family, she says.

"Page Doctor Gilman!" I yell at her, but she stares at me, confused. I pull out my phone and try my father's number, praying he'll answer.

"Sebastian?" he asks.

THE TRIAGE NURSE takes my phone and speaks to him, because I can't breathe.

Dad's there then. He's in doctor mode but concern is clear on his face. The nurse, alarmed at his presence, explains that I've asked to see a Mr Keller and yelled at her when she said no.

"Ryland's been admitted?" he asks, his eyes wide.

He pulls me along with him into the elevator and then into his office. I tell him Ryland's not in his fucking office, but my father sits me in his chair and tells me to breathe and to count.

Then he picks up his phone. Eighteen deep breaths later, he hangs up and turns to me.

———

"RYLAND'S IN SURGERY," he says. "We won't know the extent of his injuries until I speak with the surgeon."

I know Dad's talking, I can see his lips moving. But there's no sound and the room's pulsing. I'm too hot, my mouth is dry and my heartbeat's too loud.

"Sebastian? Sebastian?" my father snaps his fingers at me. "Can you hear me?"

Time, give him time, everyone said.

Time, he needs time, they urged me.

Well, now he doesn't have any fucking time.

"Will he be okay?" My tears fall at will. "Just tell me if he'll be okay."

———

THE WAITING ROOM IS CLINICAL, too damn small, and filled with Gilmans. There's no clock... it's either hospital policy or someone punched it for ticking.

Every second, every minute, is pure fucking torture.

Finally, *finally,* a woman in scrubs comes into the room and talks to my father. My brain won't let the words compute, but my brother picks me up by the shoulders and drags me down the hall.

They leave me in a room with beeping machines, a bed and a broken man.

"You've got two minutes," Dad says softly.

Time. Again, it all comes down to time.

HE LOOKS SO SMALL. He's bandaged, plastered, bruised, scraped and sleeping. He's still beautiful, even as crumpled and vulnerable as he is.

I want to touch him, but his hands are bandaged and cannulated. I trace my fingers along his fingertips, then along his bandaged brow.

My lungs hurt and my heart aches. I try to speak, but I choke on my tears and my words are only sounds.

I have an instinctual urge to wrap him up and take him away, somewhere safe, and hold him. But I can't move.

A doctor comes in and tells me it's time.

MY FATHER EXPLAINS Ryland's injuries; his leg is broken in three places, ribs fractured, spleen and kidney bruised, superficial scratches. "He was standing side-on when the van hit him," Dad says. "Most damage is to the right side of his body. His X-rays show a lot of old injuries."

"I know," I admit quietly. "He took a beating a few years ago. His workmates found out he was gay."

"Jesus Christ," Dad murmurs. My mother starts to cry.

Pressing my finger and thumb into my eyes to stem fresh tears, I pull my phone out and make a call. "Justin?"

RYLAND STIRS AND WAKES, and I am there, holding his hand. "I'm here, Ry," I tell him. I don't want him to think he's woken up in the hospital, again, with nobody there.

"Hurts," is all he says before sleep claims him again.

Later, the doctors come in and I'm ushered out. I'm told to stay out, and when my dad comes out of the room he tells me, "He's awake." But there's concern in his eyes and it scares me.

"Sebastian," Dad says softly, "he's in a lot of pain, and he... he says he wants to be alone."

———

HE'S BEEN DISTANCING himself from me since Texas. Since his father's funeral, since his mother turned on her heel and walked away from him without a word.

He's been pushing me away, in some fucked-up way of protecting himself.

I walk into the room. My heart's pounding loudly, my stomach twists. Ryland turns his face from me. "Sebastian, please go."

I'm tired, I'm so fucking tired.

But I refuse to give up, I refuse to walk away. He might not think he's worth it, he might think it's over... but he *is* worth it, and it's far from fucking over.

———

"NO." My response is immediate, my voice determined.

His eyes close tightly and he whispers drowsily, "I don't deserve you."

Although his words sting me, there is no conviction in his voice. I know what he's doing.

I walk over to him and gently take his face in my hands. He's swollen, cut and bruised and he has tears in his eyes, but I tell him anyway, "I'm not leaving you, no matter how hard you push. You are worth it, Ryland Keller, and I will fight for you."

He starts to cry then, and my tears mix with his.

———

MY FOREHEAD TOUCHES his and his sky-colored eyes haunt me, like he still doubts my words. "I'll never leave you," I tell him. "I'll tell you twenty times a day if that's what it takes."

He tries to smile, and sniffles and I wipe his tears. "Everything hurts," he whispers with a groan.

"You scared me," I whisper. "I thought I'd lost you. I was so scared. I couldn't... God, Ry, I can't live without you..."

He gently squeezes my hand and closes his eyes. He murmurs, "I'm sorry... for everything."

"Ssshhh," I hush him. "Sleep. I'm not going anywhere."

———

RYLAND SLEEPS on and off while my family comes in and out. I'm sure the hospital staff isn't impressed, but considering Dad told them Ryland's family, none of them argue.

I tell Dad that Ry's been mumbling that his leg really hurts.

"That's good," Dad says. I'm about to ask how on earth Ryland being in pain is ever *fucking good* when he explains. "Sebastian, that means he can feel his leg. He's lucky not to have spinal damage or a serious head injury."

And just like that, reality smacks me in the chest, as to how close we came...

I HEAR familiar voices outside Ryland's room and I smile. I stand up, just as Neil and Brandon come into the room. They're wide-eyed and try to smile for me, but their eyes keep flickering to the bed.

They don't say anything, but Neil puts the bouquet of flowers he's holding on the shelf.

Brandon whispers, "Holy fuck."

"He's resting," I tell them.

Neil looks at me, raising one eyebrow. "If you're gonna show us your sexy legs in work boots, Sebastian, the least you could do is wear your tool belt."

It's faint, but Ryland breathes out a chuckle.

I TURN TO FACE HIM, my broken boy, and see the corner of his lips curl. His eyes are heavy-lidded.

"You look like hell," Neil tells him. "Hasn't anyone told you being hit by a van is bad for your complexion?"

Ryland smiles then grimaces and winces.

Neil smiles sadly and apologizes with a kiss to Ryland's forehead. Brandon does the same, just as Hamish and Annie walk in. They bring more flowers with them, as does my mom.

It makes me smile.

When he wakes up, he'll know people have been here to see him. He'll know he's loved.

I FALL asleep in the chair beside the bed and when I wake up, it's morning. There's an overnight bag by my feet and there are doctors talking to Ryland and my father.

He's awake, but in a haze of morphine. He looks at me, blinks slowly, then he smiles. He looks like hell, his bruises have more color, but he's still beautiful.

They're discussing more surgery on his leg, pins and rods of some sort. They say he'll be here for at least another two weeks, followed by months of physiotherapy.

I look into his sky-blue eyes and smile.

I SHOWER in the room's bathroom, and eat the breakfast Mom brought in. Ry eats a few bites and Mom smiles. She kisses his forehead, then mine before she leaves.

That afternoon, I hear footsteps and muffled voices before Justin bursts into the room, followed by Kate.

Justin stops when he sees his brother and sucks in a breath.

Even though he's drugged up, Ryland's still surprised. Justin and Kate are quickly at his side, asking if he's okay, not sure where to touch him.

But Ryland's eyes aren't on his brother. They're on the older woman standing at the door.

RYLAND'S HELPLESS, bed-bound and vulnerable, his mouth open and his eyes stark and wide. He's breathing harder and I am concerned for his ribs and his pain. My first instinct is to protect him and I'm quickly by his side.

He squeezes my hand, silently asking me to stay, and I squeeze back to tell him I'm not going anywhere.

Justin sees how tightly Ry is holding onto me. He rests his hand on his brother's shoulder and tells him he'll be just outside.

And for the first time in two and a half years, Ryland's mother speaks to him.

"WHEN I SAW you at the funeral," she says, not bothering to wipe away her tears, "I could have sworn it was your daddy. You look so much like him."

I feel like an intruder in this conversation, but Ryland's grip on my hand tightens and his fingers tremble. His mother looks at me then, but talks to him.

"I've wished for a lot of things in my life," she says as she cries. "I wish Jim never died, I do, and I wish he never said what he said, but above all... I wish I defended my son."

RYLAND sobs then immediately winces and groans. His eyes close and he scrubs roughly at the tears on his face, hitting the gash above his eye, and he groans again.

He reaches blindly for the button which releases pain meds and presses it twice. He turns his head, but tightens his hold on my hand. "Don't go," he whispers to me. "Please don't leave me."

I turn to his mother, who looks as if she's about to fall apart, and quietly ask her to leave.

She does, and Ryland cries as sleep claims him.

He never lets go of my hand.

———

IT'S a morphine-induced sleep and he'll be out for a while. I lean over and kiss his temple, and even though he can't hear me, I tell him I'll be just outside the door.

Mrs. Keller is crying and I am reminded that she not long ago lost her husband. I can see from the three faces looking at me that Ryland is not the only Keller who has had a difficult three weeks.

Ryland's mother tries to smile as Justin and Kate both hug me. When they both look behind me, I turn to find my parents are watching.

———

MY FATHER INTRODUCES himself and explains that while he's not Ryland's doctor, he's asked to be kept informed. "He looks a lot worse than he is," he reassures them. "He has a lot of superficial wounds that'll heal nicely. But his leg is a mess and his ribs will take some time."

Justin gives my mom a sad smile. "You must be Justin," Mom says. "I can tell from your eyes." He nods and introduces Kate and his mother.

Mom composes an insincere smile for Ryland's mother, and lifts the box in her hand. "I brought *my* boys some soup."

I FOLLOW Mom into Ryland's room. "Mom, please don't add fuel to the fire. Mrs Keller just lost her husband."

Mom turns with severe eyes. "She abandoned her son!" she whispers fiercely. "I can't forgive her for that."

"Mom," I say, "it's not you, or me, who has to forgive her." I look then at the sleeping man in the bed next to us. "It's up to Ry, Mom. No one else."

"Do you think he will?" she asks, sniffling.

"I don't know. I hope so," I answer honestly, and I lean in and kiss the side of her head.

KNOWING I won't be leaving the hospital anytime soon, I offer the keys to my car and the keys to my house to Ryland's family.

It's not lost on me that Ryland's mother is about to walk into a house decorated in mementos of Ryland's life which she's had no part of: photographs of him, happy and laughing, living a life any parent should be proud of. Mementos of all she's missed.

When Ry wakes, I tell him his family will be back in the morning. Sitting on the side of his bed, I feed him spoonfuls of chicken soup.

THE NEXT DAY, three days after his accident, Ryland goes back into surgery. I take a quick shower and when I walk out of the bathroom, Justin and Kate are there, and Mrs

Keller stands to meet me. "Sebastian?" she says. "I was hoping we could talk."

"Coffee?" I suggest and we start walking to the cafeteria. "I haven't had breakfast," I say. "Ry couldn't eat before surgery, and I didn't want to eat in front of him."

"You're very good to him," she muses sadly.

I stop walking, look her in the eye and say, "Because I love him."

WE SIT with our coffee and I can see she's wrestling with her words, getting them right in her head. I wait for her to start.

She talks of when Ryland was just a boy. The things he did, the trouble he got into, the days he should have been at school but went horse-riding instead. He'd spend hours drawing instead of doing homework, but he'd do Justin's chores as well as his own so his brother wouldn't get into trouble.

I smile at the images she puts in my head and when she looks at me, she smiles too.

I NEED TO PHONE DAEVYN, so I head out and make the call. I ask for more time off and he grants it. I've had almost no vacation time in years. He tells me to call him in a week.

He tells me that OSHA and police reports have been filled out, and the witnesses have all been interviewed.

"Sebastian," he says, "the guys had Ryland's phone.

They looked through his contacts to see who they should call."

He's quiet and I know what he's about to say...

"There was a picture of you with your number... Sebastian, they know."

I SIT in Ryland's room, waiting for him to wake up, wondering what the hell I am going to tell him. His worst fear of his co-workers finding out he's gay has been realized. His father died without resolving hurtful words, he's been hit by a fucking van, he'll be off work for the better part of a year, and...

...and I wonder how much more he can take.

He stirs, but a nurse is tending to him, and he looks around, alarmed. He croaks, "Sebastian?"

The nurse pats him. "He's right here, sweetheart," she says soothingly. "He's right here."

RY RELAXES AND THE NURSE, an older woman, smiles and finishes checking his machines. When she leaves, I am quick to grab his hand. His leg, now with metal rods and pins, is under a sheet.

His eyes are closed but he lifts his hand and I press it against my cheek, rubbing my unshaven jaw. He opens one eye lazily and smirks. He mumbles, "Scruff," and I smile against his hand.

Dad comes in, checks his chart and looks in his eyes. Ry, being anaesthetically drunk, says, "I like scruff."

I laugh for the first time in three weeks.

IT'S like a weight has been lifted. The shock, the serious-ness of the accident has lessened somewhat and we're now looking forward: Ryland coming home, what he can do and what he can't.

He'll have headaches for a while, he'll be moody, frus-trated and may even go through bouts of depression, the doctor explains.

And I know that I have to tell him his workmates now know he's gay. I want him to know before he leaves the hospital. I'd prefer all the bad news to be left here, so when he goes home he can concentrate on getting better.

RYLAND and his mother skirt around each other, still waiting for Ryland to tell her either she's forgiven, or she still has only one son.

There is so much—so very much—that needs saying and finally Mrs Keller asks if she can have a moment with Ryland, alone.

"No," Ry says. "Whatever you have to say to me, you can say in front of Sebastian."

Mrs Keller swallows and nods, as Ryland continues, "Momma, I'd love nothing more than having you back in my life, but if you can't accept me for who I am, then there's no place for you."

MRS KELLER BLINKS. "RYLAND..."

"Momma, you don't understand," he says. "I'm gay. I'll always be gay. If you're expecting that to change, you're going to be disappointed." He talks calmly, confidently, which surprises me.

"I love Sebastian. I *love* him, Momma," Ryland tells her and his words warm my chest. He smiles at me. "He's everything to me."

His mother looks between us and gives a small smile.

Ryland's chin lifts and he takes a deep breath, fortified and brave. "If you want me to choose, Momma, then you *will be* disappointed, because it's him. It will always be him."

***

I'M STUNNED INTO SILENCE. I'm so proud of him, and I've never loved him more. Ryland smiles and exhales shakily.

I mouth the words *I love you* to him and he mouths, *Thank you*, back to me.

Mrs Keller looks a little out of place. I think she was honestly expecting him to forgive and forget and for life to be rosy.

Justin and Kate have no doubt heard the conversation and walk into the room, and I think the brothers could use a little alone time.

"Mrs Keller, coffee?"

SHE NODS AND SMILES GRATEFULLY. "Please, Sebastian, call me Maggie."

Sitting across from each other, with our coffees between us, this time it's me who talks. "Mrs Keller... Maggie, Ryland is very good at pushing people away for fear of being hurt again. I should know... he tried that with me. But I proved to him that I love him, by fighting for him."

She looks at me and I can see traces of Ryland in her face. "I hurt him so badly," she says quietly.

"Then prove to him you're sorry. Prove to him you love him. If you want your son back, then don't quit. Fight for him."

WE WALK BACK into Ryland's room to three smiling faces, though Ry looks tired. He glances at me, silently curious as to my conversation with his mother. I give him a smile that tells him it's okay.

"You're tired," I say. "You should sleep. How's your headache? Can I get a doctor for you?"

"I'm okay," he says with a smile. "I'm actually waiting for your mom. She was making me stew with dumplings..."

"Sleep, Ry," I suggest. "I'll wake you when she gets here."

When I kiss his forehead, his eyes close and he falls asleep with a smile.

ON THE THIRD day after his surgery, he's eating breakfast

and I'm reading a newspaper when Dad comes in with another doctor. "Ryland, you're going to walk for us today," my doctor father says.

Ryland looks at him and snorts. "You're much funnier making jokes at Hamish's expense, Douglas."

"I'm serious, Ryland." Dad uses his doctor voice.

Ryland looks at him, then at me with wide blue eyes. "I can't. I mean, I don't think"

The other doctor cuts him off. "Ryland, you're not going home until you try."

Ry pushes his tray away. "Why didn't you just say that?"

MINDFUL OF HIS OTHER INJURIES, the two doctors hold Ryland and he tentatively puts his feet to the floor. They let him sit for a while, letting his head get used to being upright.

He takes hold of their arms and I can see his knuckles are white.

His flame-blue eyes look at me, starkly declaring he can't do this.

Dad sees this silent exchange and, standing with his hands on Ryland's arms, he says, "Ryland, it's okay. I've got you, son."

Ryland looks up at my father for a long moment, then nods. He holds on, and he stands.

HIS KNUCKLES ARE WHITE, he's holding on so tight. I

know how strong those hands are.

He grimaces at the pain in his side, in his head, in his leg. But he grits his teeth and hisses, his forehead beading with sweat.

I have to stop myself from going to him, helping him, or yelling at my father to leave him the fuck alone.

But it's Ryland's determination, his resolve to never let anything beat him that makes him do it.

Four steps.

Four steps, that's all, and Dad grins, telling him it's enough. "I told them you'd do it."

THEY SETTLE Ryland back into his bed and he's pale, exhausted. His doctor asks him how he feels and Ryland barks a short laugh, daring him to guess.

Dad hands him a paper cup with pills and one of water. He takes them with shaky hands and swallows them down. He falls back against his pillows, his eyes closed, and surely his harsh breathing is hurting his ribs.

I take his hand and kiss his forehead, as salt water slips from the corners of his eyes.

I wipe his tears, wishing I could absorb his pain. "You did great, Ry."

I smile as I hear their voices approach the room. I know what their reactions will be. Neil and Brandon walk into Ryland's room. And stop.

"WELL, MMM-MMM," Neil hums. Brandon's mouth

opens.

Fighting a laugh, I make introductions. "Neil, Brandon, this is Justin."

Justin stands, all jeans, boots and sky-colored eyes. Brandon studies Ryland's brother, mentally undressing him before extending his hand.

From his bed, Ryland says, "Sorry, boys. He's straight," just as Justin and Brandon shake hands.

Brandon sighs. "So disappointing." Neil tsks. Justin blushes a kaleidoscope of pink.

"For you maybe." Kate laughs, standing to meet them.

"AND YOU MUST BE MRS KELLER." Neil oozes charm. "How did you manage two such beautiful boys?"

It's now her turn to blush. "They get their looks from their daddy."

"Well, eye color maybe," Neil says. "But their Southern manners and those pretty dimples are what gave you away."

Ryland's mother smiles genuinely and looks to everyone. "Can I get anyone anything?"

Brandon brightens. "Another gay son, if you have one."

I resist the urge to groan, but Mrs Keller surprises us by laughing. "He'd be no use to you, sugar. It seems my sons have a thing for blonds."

WHEN IT COMES time for the Kellers to leave, I offer Ry and his mother some alone time.

"No, please, Sebastian," Maggie says, "this involves

you too."

Ryland reaches for my hand and I take it, waiting to hear what his mother has to say.

"I want you to know you're more than welcome to visit me at any time. You both are."

"I can't just forget what my father said to me," Ryland counters.

"Sorry won't ever atone for what *he*, for what *we*, said and did," Maggie says tearfully. "But you *are* my son and I love you."

"MOM..." Ryland starts.

"Ryland, honey," his mom interrupts. "I really am sorry. I don't expect you to forgive me easily, but I thought over time... I was hoping you, and Sebastian, would like to visit." She smiles at us. "Both of you. Like a family."

Ryland holds his head high. Hope and tears brim in his eyes. "You mean that?"

Mrs Keller nods. "Of course I do." She leans in, kisses his cheeks and whispers, "He's a good man. I can see how much he loves you. How could I not like anyone who thinks my boy hung the moon?"

JUSTIN HUGS RY for the longest time. "I'll call Sebastian to let you know we get home okay," Kate says. "But if we want to make this flight, we really have to go."

Justin told me he'll never forgive himself for not visiting

Ry the first time he was in the hospital. He's certainly made up for it now.

When Maggie kisses Ryland's cheek, he tells her to call. She smiles through tears and nods. He's offering an olive branch and she knows it.

When they've gone, Ry leans back against his pillows. It's only mid-afternoon, he's exhausted—physically, emotionally—but he smiles.

I BARELY GET to kiss him properly when a nurse walks in. "Good afternoon!" she says brightly. "Shower before dinner?"

Ry keeps his eyes on me—he looks kiss-drunk—not hearing the nurse at all.

I smile. "Shower?"

"Mmmm, yes, please," he murmurs.

When the nurse laughs, Ry's surprised she's in his room. "Oh, um, yeah, I guess," he says, disappointed.

"I could do it!" I say. "I'll be the one helping him at home, it's probably best if I start now."

She rolls her eyes. "Didn't your doctor tell you?"

"Tell me what?" Ry asks.

"No... *sexual relations*... for four weeks."

"FOUR WEEKS?" I'm not sure which one of us asks the loudest just as Dad walks into the room.

"Four weeks for what?"

The nurse answers, "No fooling around."

"Ahhh." Dad smiles knowingly, looking through Ry's charts.

"Douglas," Ry says pleadingly. "Four weeks? Please! I broke my leg, not my di—"

Dad raises his hand, interrupting Ry's words. "And four ribs, cuts, bruises, mild concussion, bruised spleen and kidney —you were damn lucky not to have serious organ trauma."

"Four weeks *is* serious organ trauma," Ry mutters.

I laugh and my father tries not to smile. "Four weeks won't kill you."

"RYLAND, WHAT ARE YOU DOING?" Dad asks, as Ry tries to get himself up.

"Sebastian's going to help me shower," he says.

"Oh, no, he's not," Dad replies.

"Oh, yes, he is," I tell him.

"Sebastian, considering what's just been said about abstinence, I don't think that's a good idea."

"Well," I argue, "considering I'll be helping him at home, I think it's a good idea."

Ry grins. "I think it's a *great* idea."

Determined, he puts his feet on the floor, wincing as he does. I gently pull his left arm around my shoulder, getting him to his feet.

LOWERING HIM INTO A SHOWER CHAIR, I pull his gown off. I run the shower and let the water stream down his shoulders while I get undressed.

He's naked and wet, and my cock is aching. It's been so long since he touched me, since before his father's funeral. I can see he's hard too.

I stand in front of him. I know he sees my erection, but his eyes don't leave mine.

Taking the shower nozzle, I wash him down. I am mindful of his injuries, his bruises, his sutures, and he stares at me with those azure eyes.

HIS HAND REACHES SLOWLY and his fingers thread with mine. He lowers our joined hands and wraps my hand around his cock.

He whimpers and gasps at the contact, his blue eyes flutter closed.

I clip the shower nozzle back into place and grip him properly. I squeeze him, pump him.

I grip my own cock and pump myself, quick, hard. I jerk us both off, wet, slick and swollen.

"Tell me if it hurts," I pant.

He groans. "Hurts. So. Fucking. Good."

I come hard, so hard. Ryland's cries sound more pain than pleasure, but his cock erupts regardless.

HE'S UTTERLY SPENT and although he denies it, I can tell he's in pain.

I try to wash his hair but he's got stitches in his head. I try to wash his leg but he's got two rows of staples, one in his thigh, one down his shin.

I dry him, somewhat clumsily. I get him dressed again, apologizing the entire time.

I wrap a towel around my waist and slowly help him into bed. He leans back, hurt and exhausted. "That was great," he groans. "But I don't think we should try that again for... oh, about four weeks."

———

THE NEXT MORNING, Ry and I are finally alone. I have to tell him that everyone at work knows he's gay, they know I'm gay, they know we're together. I can't put it off any longer.

He takes the news well. Too well.

"It doesn't matter," he says simply. "I'm not going back."

"What?"

"I can't work anyway, with my leg and all." He shrugs. "Justin signed the paperwork for my half of my father's will. He reckons I should use the old bastard's money to go to college. I'll be the best *queer faggot architect* just to spite him."

———

"I HAVEN'T EVEN LOOKED into it," he says. "I don't even know when the semester starts." But he's bright and excited.

"Oh, Ry," I say with a smiling kiss. "You'll be the best queer faggot architect *ever*."

He snorts, but I can tell his memories have returned to his father by the faraway look in his eyes. "So, what are you going to do?"

"What do you mean?"

"Well, you can't go back to work if they *know*." His tone is serious, quiet. "No fucking way."

I haven't time to respond before my phone beeps with a message from Daevyn.

"I NEED TO CALL HIM," I tell Ry.

"And tell him what?"

I understand his trepidation, I do. But I have a mortgage. "Ry, I need to go back."

His glare hardens and his whole frame tenses, making him grimace. "You can't go back onto that site, not by yourself, not ever. If something were to happen..."

"Ry, it'll be okay."

"No!" he barks loudly. "Goddammit, Sebastian, no!"

My doctor father walks in and demands to know what's going on.

Ry hisses, "Unless you want your son in a bed here beside me, try to talk some sense into him."

RY GOES from livid to pleading. "Please, Seb. Please."

Dad looks between us, then his eyes stop on me. "Sebastian, you haven't been home in a week. You should go."

"I'm not leaving," I say.

"I'm not asking," Dad says. "I'm telling you."

Ryland won't look at me, so I sit on the side of the bed and rest my forehead against his. "Dad's kicking me out," I say with a pout.

Ryland's lips twitch, fighting a smile. Then his sky-colored eyes meet mine, a shade of haunted blue. "If something were to happen to you, I'd never forgive myself."

I WALK INTO OUR HOUSE. It's quiet, empty. The Kellers have left it as they found it. It's tidy, clean even. Everything is where it should be.

But something's missing.

I attempt to eat, but my appetite's gone. My argument with Ry is lumped in my stomach instead. I wander aimlessly through each room. Something's missing. I search, looking for what's not there, why it doesn't feel like home.

It's because my home isn't here. My home is lying in hospital, and he's worth more than any job.

I take out my phone, scroll for Daevyn's number, and hit dial.

I BRING Ryland coffee and croissants and he's awake when I walk in. I've missed him. So fucking much. It's only been one night and I wonder how I existed before I knew him.

His blue eyes, his entire face, brightens when he sees me. "I'm sorry," he says. "I don't want to fight with you."

"I'm sorry too." I'm so, so sorry. I peck his lips. "I didn't mean to upset you."

He smiles and sighs. "I spoke to your dad when you left," he says. "He's right. If you want to go back to work, then you should."

"RY, I know you'll be worried sick every day I walk out the door," I say. "I don't want you to worry."

"Of course I will," he replies. "I'll try *not* to, but, I just... what I went through..."

"That's why I'm not going back."

He stares at me. "But you love your job."

"I love you more," I counter. "You mean more to me than a job. I know how strongly you feel about this, Ry. I can't ignore that. I won't."

He's quiet for a long moment. "What will you do?"

I answer honestly. "I have no idea."

HE WHISPERS, "I don't want you to resent me if it's not what you want."

"I can't resent you when it's my decision." I sigh. "Ry, I got home last night and all I could think about was you, about us. Our home isn't our home without you... my life isn't a life without you."

"Oh," he breathes.

"You can't spend your days worrying if I'll be safe, or when the phone rings if it'll be *that* kind of phone call," I say. "I won't put you through that. Never again."

Those sky-colored eyes fill with tears and he nods.

WITH A FULL-TIME CAREGIVER and Dad promising

to keep an eye on him, we're given the okay to bring Ry home.

The sofa has replaced the hospital bed, the coffee table now his bed tray. I keep everything within his reach so he maintains as much independence as possible. I can see when he needs to do things for himself, or when he's getting frustrated and angry, and then I'll help him.

But he's happier at home.

I'm happier now he's home.

When Ry's been home for two days, I tell my mom about my plans to quit my job.

"ARE YOU SURE, SEBASTIAN?" Mom asks.

I look at Ryland. I have no doubt. "I'm sure."

"What about your mortgage?" she continues.

"I have some money saved and I can re-draw on my loan if I have to," I tell her. "It's only temporary. Just until I decide what it is I'll be doing."

"I have money," Ry interrupts.

"I'm not using your college money, Ry," I say. "Thanks for offering, but you need that."

He frowns and scowls at me, so I quickly add, "We'll get you up on your feet before I have to worry about that anyway."

"CAN you grab me the legal stuff that Justin left me?" Ry asks.

"Sure," I say, finding the large yellow envelope he's

after, and hand it to him.

He pulls out papers, and when he finds the one he's after, he hands it to me. "Read that."

I take the document. It's legal jargon I can't understand, but there are dollar figures at the bottom, under the title "Transferee."

But I understand one thing.

Justin James Keller transferred a fucking lot of money to Ryland James Keller.

RY SMILES at my gaping mouth. "I told you I had some money."

I shake my head, trying to process this information, but Ry won't be deterred. "You can use the money to set up your own business," he says. "Or go to college? Whatever you want." He beams of endless possibilities. "You once told me I could have the best of both worlds. Well, you can too."

"Ry," I start, not sure what to say.

"You love building. You love design and function," he says. "If you can make your dream job a reality, you should."

I blink.

Then he adds, "If I could make your dream job a reality, I will."

"I CAN'T TAKE YOUR MONEY," I say, handing him back the papers. "It's yours."

"Stop being so damn proud," he snaps. "I'm the reason

you're not working, I won't let you lose your house."

"It won't get to that," I say, but truthfully, I'm not sure it won't.

"Damn straight it won't get to that." He huffs. "Sebastian, I want you to take some of it, all of it, I don't care."

"I care," I say. "I'm not arguing with you about money, Ry. Please drop it."

"There is one way that I can make you take it," he says.

"WHAT'RE YOU TALKING ABOUT?" I ask.

"You keep saying 'it's yours, it's not mine,' well, there's one way to fix that."

My silence and expectant gaze prompt him to keep talking. He grins. "We could make it *ours*."

I roll my eyes, not understanding what he means. But Mom seems to get something I don't, because her eyes bug out and she starts to buzz.

Ryland, from his perch on the sofa, looks at her and laughs.

"Ry, what do you mean, 'make it ours?'"

And for the longest moment, he stares at me with those sky-colored eyes. "Marry me."

"RYLAND," I whisper. I can't take my eyes off him. My heart beats double-time.

A bubble of excitement escapes from Mom, but she clamps her hands over her mouth.

"Sebastian, without you, I have nothing," Ry says so

goddamn calmly. "Can you live without me?"

"No."

"Will you ever want anyone else?"

"No."

"Will you ever leave dirty clothes on the floor?"

I snort. "No."

"Will you ever leave wet towels on the bed?"

I smile. "No."

"Will you ever eat all the frozen boysenberry yoghurt without me?"

I laugh. "No."

His beautiful eyes shine. "Will you marry me?"

"Yes."

MOM SQUEALS AND JUMPS, then squeals some more before she tackle-hugs me. It's the quickest embrace from her *ever*, because the next second she's lean-hugging Ry as he sits on the sofa. Then she's bouncing, grabbing her bag, punching numbers into her cell as she races out the door. I haven't even blinked.

"I think your mom's excited," Ry says, smiling.

I straddle him, keeping my weight on my knees. I lean in and kiss him soundly until he hums.

"Married, huh?" I murmur against his lips.

"One condition," he says. "We wait until I can *walk* down the aisle."

THREE WEEKS LATER

RYLAND SITS on the dining chair, a pillow at his back, his slowly healing leg splayed straight and to the side. He's naked. His cock is swollen, bulging.

I am standing over him, naked, fucking his mouth as his fingers probe my ass. He's fucking me with his fingers, thrusting into me as I thrust into him.

He takes my cock, long and deep, into his throat. He sucks and moans and I hold his head, fisting his hair as his fingers prep me. And I come. Hot, thick spurts rip pleasure from my skin, from my bones.

And he drinks.

His head falls back. I lean my head on his shoulder and I lower myself onto his cock. I am so full of him. Every inch of him.

He's breathing harder and when he's fully seated inside me, he shudders.

"Does it hurt?" I ask.

He shakes his head. "I'm gonna come already."

Groaning, I roll my hips and his eyes roll back in his

head. He grips my hips and it feels so good to have him hold me, fill me.

I kiss him, taking his tongue in my mouth, and as he grunts, I can feel his cock swell.

He desperately grabs my jaw, my neck, anywhere he can reach, and he kisses me. Hard.

I grind down on his cock and take everything he gives me, in my ass, in my mouth.

He swells inside me, lurching, hot and heavy. With a strangled cry into my mouth, he fills the condom, thrusting up into me as he does.

He shudders and flexes, moaning as his entire body riding his orgasm high.

I kiss his lips, his face, his jaw, his neck. When his blue eyes slowly open, I ask him how he feels.

He answers. One word. "Loved."

EIGHT MONTHS LATER

RYLAND POV

Sebastian finally admitted to me that the idea of designing, then building his own creations, was something he'd only ever dreamed of.

"We could go to college together," he'd suggested. "Design, then build. From conception to completion." His excitement was contagious as his plans took shape. His plans for us. "Our jobs would be personalized, detailed. Together, we'd be a dream team."

I'd laughed and told him we already were.

So the plan was to get through school then go out on our own, build our own business. If I ever doubted my ability, or my self-worth, I didn't anymore.

"Hey," Ben says. "Where's Sebastian?"

"He's just gone to grab my book," I tell him, settling into my seat, my right leg still stiff and sore. "I left it in the car. Quicker for him to go get it than me." I nod to my leg.

"Still gives you grief, yeah?" he asks.

"Yeah. Physio said it will for some time."

He grimaces sympathetically and starts talking about his girlfriend, Estela.

I like Ben. And Juan and Emilio, the other guys we hang out with at college. They're fresh outta high school and not once did they bat an eyelid that we're gay, together... married.

We've been at college now for two months. We've kinda buddied up with Ben and his mates. To them, we're just two ordinary, albeit older, guys. They help us with study, timetables, classes. We help them with the principles of construction.

Sebastian comes into the lecture room, windswept and fucking gorgeous from running. He takes his seat beside me, hands me my book, and smiles.

Sebastian asks Ben how Estela's doing and all Ben says is, "Be thankful you two don't have to listen to girly shit like makeup, heels and handbags."

Yep. I like him.

Sebastian and I both laugh.

God, how different my life is now. How different I am now. The things Sebastian has taught me... the things he's shown me, proved to me, allowed me to be. That when two worlds, the best of both worlds, collide, it's a rare and beautiful thing.

It hasn't *all* been sunshine and rainbows. But I'd take a lifetime of the shittiest days with Sebastian over one day without him.

The professor comes in and starts taking roll call.

"Gilman-Keller, Ryland?"

"Here."

"Gilman-Keller, Sebastian?"

I smile. Every. Fucking. Time.

Sebastian looks at me and grins. "Here."

$\sim$ The End $\sim$

ABOUT THE AUTHOR

N.R. Walker is an Australian author, who loves her genre of gay romance. She loves writing and spends far too much time doing it, but wouldn't have it any other way.

She is many things: a mother, a wife, a sister, a writer. She has pretty, pretty boys who live in her head, who don't let her sleep at night unless she gives them life with words. She likes it when they do dirty, dirty things... but likes it even more when they fall in love.

She used to think having people in her head talking to her was weird, until one day she happened across other writers who told her it was normal.

She's been writing ever since...

Contact N.R. Walker

nrwalker.net
Email:
nrwalker@nrwalker.net

ALSO BY N.R. WALKER

TITLES IN AUDIO:

Red Dirt Heart 4

The Weight Of It All

Switched

Point of No Return

Breaking Point

Starting Point

Spencer Cohen Book One

Spencer Cohen Book Two

Spencer Cohen Book Three

Yanni's Story : Spencer Cohen Book Four

On Davis Row

Evolved

Free Reads:

Sixty Five Hours

Learning to Feel

His Grandfather's Watch (And The Story of Billy and Hale)

The Twelfth of Never (Blind Faith 3.5)

Twelve Days of Christmas (Sixty Five Hours Christmas)

Best of Both Worlds

Translated Titles:

Fiducia Cieca (Italian translation of Blind Faith)

Attraverso Questi Occhi (Italian translation of Through